In memory of Ted,
who believed in the book,

and Scott,
who inspired the story.

www.mascotbooks.com

Blue Toboggan

©2016 Joanna H. Kraus. All Rights Reserved. No part of this publication may be reproduced, stored in a retrieval system or transmitted in any form by any means electronic, mechanical, or photocopying, recording or otherwise without the permission of the author.

For more information, please contact:
Mascot Books
560 Herndon Parkway #120
Herndon, VA 20170
info@mascotbooks.com

Library of Congress Control Number: 2016917431

CPSIA Code: PRT1216A
ISBN-13: 978-1-63177-836-0

Printed in the United States

Blue
TOBOGGAN

by Joanna H. Kraus
Illustrated by Chiara Savarese

Together.

We did everything together,
From kindergarten...until three months ago.
Me and Will. Will and me.
Soccer, swimming, rock climbing.
When he won a school prize for his story, I cheered.
When I made my first soccer goal, he jumped up and down yelling, "Spectacular!"
That was his favorite word ever since he won the class spelling bee with it.
Our big dream was a blue toboggan to *whoosh* down Wildberry Hill come winter.
We both saw it at the same time
In the Sports World window.

SPECTACULAR!!!

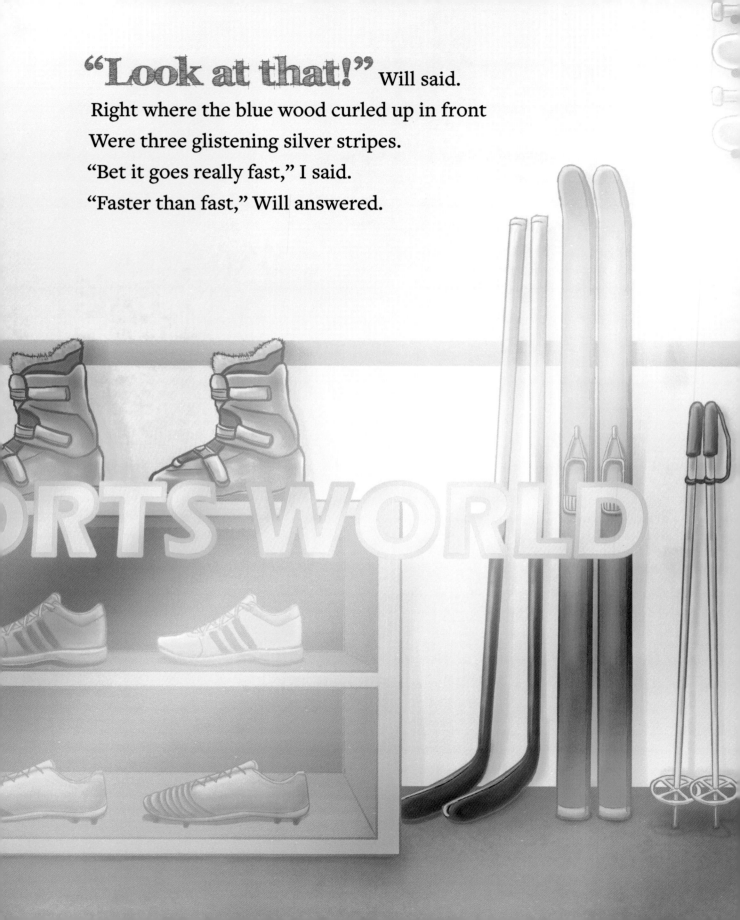

"Look at that!" Will said.
Right where the blue wood curled up in front
Were three glistening silver stripes.
"Bet it goes really fast," I said.
"Faster than fast," Will answered.

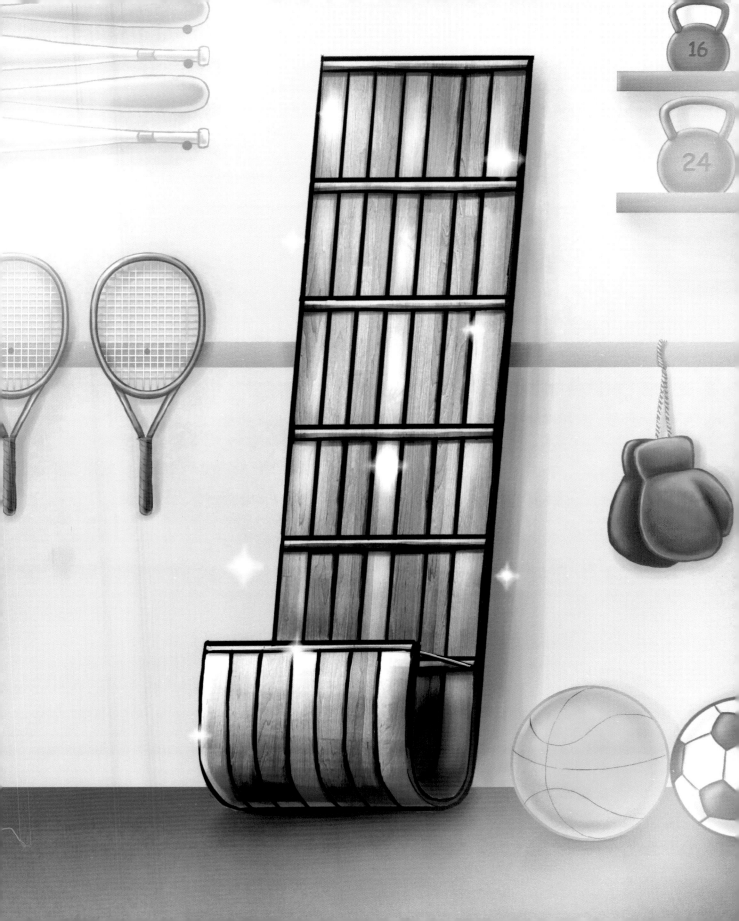

We were saving up to buy it.

The two of us,

Raking leaves and walking dogs.

Every Friday we'd count the money.

We stored it in a coffee can at the back of my closet.

"Close, Danny," he said the last time we counted.

"Really close," I said.

Soon, we'd fly down Wildberry Hill,
The two of us,

Faster than FAST

Now, my favorite ice cream doesn't taste the same.

Jokes aren't as funny.

At school there's an empty red chair where he used to sit.

Even though the teacher moved it, I know where it is.

I put a piece of bubble gum on the bottom,

And no one's found it yet.

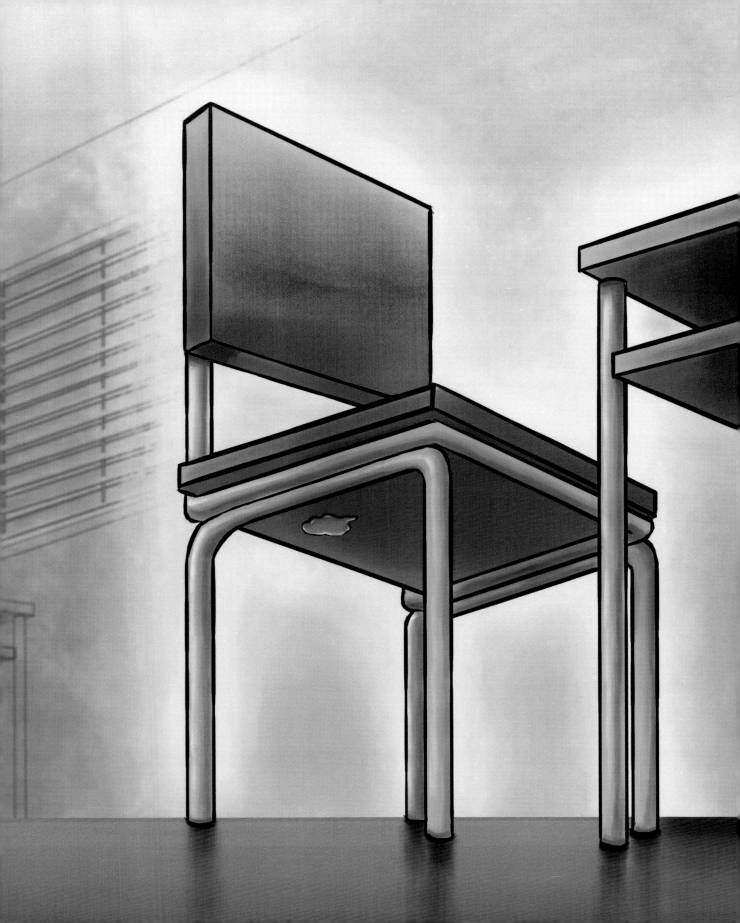

Sometimes I want to
  punch everybody who's laughing,
Pull down the shade to shut out the sun.
In my room I put on music and bang my
  drum loud
So no one will know
I'm crying.
Mom looks worried when I can't eat the
  corn pudding
She made especially for me.
Dad squeezes my shoulder and says,
"Finding new friends doesn't mean
  forgetting the old."
But I don't want to ride the blue
  toboggan without Will,
Even though the silver stripes still shine.

One morning when the daffodils are bright yellow spears on the lawn
And the grass is greener than green,
Our teacher flings the window wide open singing, "It's spring!"
Everyone laughs,
Except me.
She lets the fresh air fan our faces,
Then turns and looks at me.

"Danny," she says softly, "we all miss Will.
How do you want to remember him?"
We decide to plant a tree
In front of the school.
"Not the kind where the leaves fall off," I say.
"It's gotta be green year round."

So we have a bake sale and a car wash.
And when I bring in the toboggan money Will and I saved,
The teacher counts the coins.

"Now there's enough,"

she says and smiles at me.

We go to the nursery at the edge of town.
The clerk points to a small, dark tree.
"That balsam fir over there. One day it'll
    be as tall as your school."
I like that.
I like the idea that
Every day
I'll see
Will's tree soar to the sky.

On planting day, the music teacher plays his guitar
And we sing some of Will's favorite songs.
The bronze plaque reads, "In memory of Will."

Beside it there's a freshly dug hole.

At first the tree tilts.

But as I pack more earth in, I whisper,

"This is for you, Will."

Right away the balsam fir straightens.

IN MEMORY OF
WILL

Then we each say something about him.

How he could make funny faces that made you laugh.

How he could eat two whole pieces of chocolate cake,

But if you forgot your lunch, he'd give you half of his.

How he could imitate a robot or an astronaut on the moon,

And was the fastest runner in the room.

How he loved to make up stories.

"What I remember most,"

I say, "is the way he'd jump up and down
Whenever he was excited and yell, 'Spectacular!'"
At the end of the ceremony, Will's dad says, "Thank you."
Will's mom adds, "Will thanks you too, wherever he may be."
His dad looks up at the sun-filled sky and whispers, "There."

Today I biked to the top of Wildberry Hill
And stopped by the weeping willow.
We always came here to swap secrets and sandwiches.
It was our favorite spot.
I'll remember Will.
Today, tomorrow,
And all the days after tomorrow.

But when I do,
He'll be riding
A blue toboggan with silver stripes,
Swooping past the stars,
Racing around the moon, shouting,

"SPECTACULAR!"

About the Author

Joanna H. Kraus is an award-winning playwright of eighteen produced and published plays. *THE ICE WOLF* (Dramatic Publishing) and *REMEMBER MY NAME* (Samuel French) were both produced off-off Broadway. The former appears in several anthologies and has a Spanish version. Her latest script *Me2* is scheduled to tour Spring 2017. Kraus received the Charlotte Chorpenning Cup and the Distinguished Play Award from the American Alliance for Theatre and Education. She's written numerous articles, interviews, and reviews for the media. In addition, she's received commissions to dramatize history, among them *SUNDAY GOLD* and *ANGEL IN THE NIGHT* (Dramatic Publishing). Picture books include *A NIGHT OF TAMALES AND ROSES* (Shenanigan Books) listed in the Bank Street College of Education edition of Best Children's Books. Currently, she's Correspondent for the Bay Area News Group and the Southern California News Group and is a member of The Dramatists Guild and SCBWI. Kraus is Professor Emerita of the College at Brockport State University of New York, a graduate of Sarah Lawrence College, and holds an M.A. from UCLA and an Ed.D. from Columbia University. She lives in northern California. Her website is: www.joannakraus.com.